The Last Day of Kindergarten

by **Nancy Loewen**   illustrated by **Sachiko Yoshikawa**

SCHOLASTIC INC.
New York Toronto London Auckland
Sydney Mexico City New Delhi Hong Kong

ISBN 978-0-545-47261-6

Text copyright © 2011 by Nancy Loewen.
Illustrations copyright © 2011 by Sachiko Yoshikawa.
All rights reserved. Published by Scholastic Inc., 557 Broadway, New York, NY 10012,
by arrangement with Marshall Cavendish Corporation.
SCHOLASTIC and associated logos are trademarks and/or
registered trademarks of Scholastic Inc.

12 11 10 9 8 7 6 5 4 3   12 13 14 15 16 17/0

Printed in the U.S.A.   08

First Scholastic printing, May 2012

The illustrations were rendered digitally in mixed media.
Editor: Robin Benjamin

For my daughter, Helena, whose tearful and triumphant
last day of kindergarten inspired this story
—N.L.

To Kinu and all her friends in the Sunshine Garden
Special thanks to Mikako Miyazaki
—S.Y.

Today is the last day of kindergarten.

I wish it were the FIRST. Then I'd meet
Mrs. Popinski all over again.

I'd hang my very own backpack on my very own hook.

My markers would be bright and inky. My crayons would be pointy and new.

If it were the FIRST day of kindergarten, I'd have so much to look forward to this year.

I'd play House or Grocery Store during Creative Playtime.

I'd dress up as a tiger for the Halloween parade.

**I'd lose my first tooth biting into
Sammy McGregor's birthday cupcakes.**

But today is the LAST day of kindergarten.
We don't read stories. We don't work on our
numbers or letters. Instead, we wash the tables.

We throw out the stubbiest crayons and the dried-up paints.

We take our pictures off the walls.

Mrs. Popinski gathers us into a circle for Sharing Time. It's the last time we'll ever sit criss-cross applesauce together.

"I am so proud of all of you," Mrs. Popinski says. "You've learned so much this year! But kindergarten is ending. Summer is beginning. What are your favorite things about summer?"

Staying up late

Swimming

Picnics in the park

Running through the sprinkler

Eating blue raspberry ice pops on the front steps

"Let's talk about first grade," Mrs. Popinski says. "What are you looking forward to the most?"

Eating lunch in the cafeteria

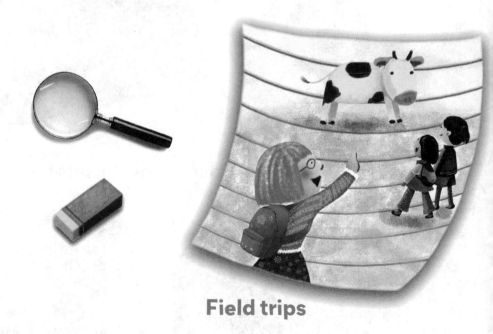

Field trips

Writing stories

Recess

Making new friends

Playing on the big kids' playground

"Wow," Mrs. Popinski says. "You're going to be fantastic first graders. I can just tell." She looks at the clock and stands up. "Okay, class. It's time!"

We put on the funny flat hats that we
made out of poster board and yarn.
We make sure our faces are clean.
 Then we line up and walk down the
hall to the auditorium.

I peek over Mason's shoulder and see a crowd—people pointing cameras at the stage, little brothers and sisters squirming on laps.

Oh! I see Mommy and Daddy! And Grandma and Grandpa and Aunt Dee. This afternoon they're going to take me out for ice cream, and I can order whatever I want.

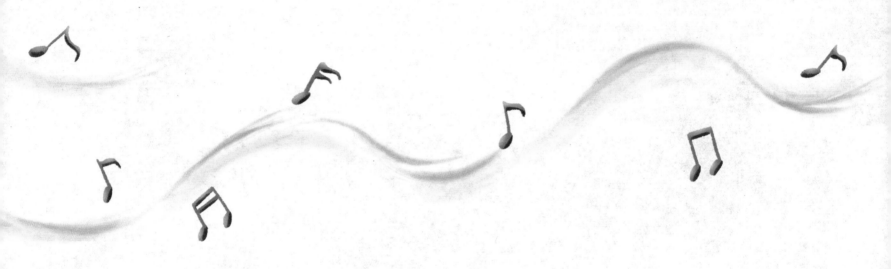

Mr. Meyer starts playing a serious song on the piano. It makes me want to cry. It makes me want to march.

It makes me want to stand up straight and tall.

This is it.

I'm walking onto the stage.

I'm reciting our ABC farewell poem without making any mistakes. I'm singing "Zip-A-Dee-Doo-Dah" and clapping in all the right places.

I'm shaking hands with the principal.

Kindergarten
is
over. . . .

I did it!

First grade, here I come!